RED
JASPER

RED JASPER

MARK RIDLER

LitPrime Solutions
21250 Hawthorne Blvd
Suite 500, Torrance, CA 90503
www.litprime.com
Phone: 1 (209) 788-3500

Published by LitPrime Solutions   05/19/2021

ISBN: 978-1-954886-55-1(sc)
ISBN: 978-1-954886-56-8(e)

Library of Congress Control Number: 2021910022

TABLE OF CONTENTS

THE PANIC OVER HINKLEY POINT

In 2017, a technician at Hinkley Point nuclear power station in the UK reported in a particle physics journal that radioactive decay events were not randomly distributed. Rather they were clustered on a statistical basis around a one hertz signal. Results were presented and corresponded to a five sigma detection.

The initial reaction was disbelief, particularly since nobody could reproduce the results. "This is the Cold Fusion scandal all over again" was the overriding sentiment.

But Hinkley Point stuck to their guns and invited selected experts to verify the results on site.

After a very small list of attendees, Theofanes Raptor was called in to investigate.

The crowds were gathered outside the perimeter fence at Hinkley Point. Clearly word had got out. "DEATH FROM 1 HZ" read the placards. "1 HZ = BOOM". "CLOSE HINKLEY POINT". Theo was mildly perturbed.

The police didn't know what to do. Aside from enforcing a peaceful protest, they were just as worried about the implications as the protesters. A run-away incident like Chernobyl seemed like a real possibility.

Theo was given special clearance for the main laboratory where he was greeted by the technician who had written the paper, Arthur Bentham.

"Pleased to meet you, Theo", he said. "Did you have a good journey?"

"Not too bad, give or take the protestors".

"Would you like to sit down? There's a brief whiteboard presentation, after which there will be an opportunity to see the results in action."

"So when did this first start happening?" Theo asked.

"About two weeks ago. It came out of nowhere. At least that was the first time we noticed anything."

"Where did you see it happening?"

"We saw it in the lab where there's immediate feedback from the monitors. The main reactor is probably seeing the same thing but we can't tell from the existing set up."

The presentation went ahead much as expected. When it came to the results, Theo could hear the clicks on the Geiger Counter as clear as daylight. His first thought was of Henning Horlicks and Kingsley Khan. "I'm going to have to report back."

He got on the phone to his boss, Julia Barnes.

"Julia, this thing is black and white. Given that I'm sat right next to a nuclear reactor, it's quite frightening really."

"I see," said Julia. "So the crowds are justified in calling for the closure of Hinkley Point?"

"Yes," he replied. "I'd like to have Henning and Kingsley in on this one."

"That's difficult because they're both working in the private sector," she replied.

"I'll leave that with you then," said Theo, knowing full well the urgency of the situation would attract them anyway.

Within the space of 24 hours, Julia had spoken to both Henning and Kingsley and they arranged flights to Bristol airport, which was the closest. They arrived within an hour of each other and shared a taxi to Hinkley Point.

"Good to see you again," said Henning.

"It's been three years," replied Kingsley. "Different world now."

"This is different again. Nuclear physics doesn't do synchronised swimming. Finding the source of the clustering will be key," continued Henning.

"Any ideas?" asked Kingsley.

"It could be a hoax. Or it could be the real thing. The one hertz signal sounds suspiciously man-made. An atomic clock sounds just the ticket," summarised Henning.

They arrived at Hinkley Point and were escorted inside where Theo was waiting.

"Gentlemen it's a pleasure to be working with you again," said Theo.

"Likewise," said Henning.

"Me too," added Kingsley. "Can you show us the way?"

Once they were inside Theo gave Henning and Kingsley a quick tour. This is the main turbine hall. The control room viewing gallery is this way.

"This is a Magnox reactor, right?" said Henning. "Has anyone tried to measure that specifically rather than the site as a whole?"

"Think we're the first to think beyond the lab," replied Theo. He was holding his head in his hands. "I really don't know what to do. I'd recommend keeping the power station running while we do further tests, but on the other hand I don't want to be stood next to it if it is going to go off."

"Nothing like putting your life on the line," said Henning.

"Let's leave the decision making to the politicians. That's what they're paid for. We should focus 100% on the tests," said Kingsley.

"What are we going to do then?" asked Theo.

"Bring in some independent kit and measure the results inside," said Henning.

"Then go walkabout outside," said Kingsley.

"Just randomly?" queried Theo.

"No, in a measured circle around the power station. If there is any directional signal in the background, we should pick it up this way," Kingsley replied. "Assuming we've got sensitive enough kit."

"Then what?"

"Depends entirely on what we get from the first round of tests".

The Mongols, as the trio were known, decided to start from scratch with their own equipment. They used Geiger-Muller tubes as radiation detectors and then interfaced with computers to make the analysis relative to a one hertz signal.

Initially they worked for three days and nights while the politicians debated.

Theresa May was holding an emergency meeting in Downing Street to discuss the potential shutdown of Hinkley Point.

"If we do shut it down, it will cause power outages across thousands of homes in the South West. You can't just take a base power station out of circulation and expect nothing to happen," said asked Amber Rudd, the home secretary. "Can we buy in some extra power from the French?".

"Depends on how much you want and how quickly." said Boris Johnson, the foreign secretary. "A full nuclear power station's worth could probably be brought online within a week or so."

"We don't have that long," said Theresa May. "I favour shutting it down sooner rather than later because nobody wants the risk of another Chernobyl."

"We don't know for certain that the source of the signal originates with the power station itself or elsewhere as part of the background. I'd recommend further tests before we make any drastic decisions," said the scientific adviser.

"Agreed," said Theresa. "We'll go ahead with the tests anyway but I reserve the right to pull the plug on Hinkley Point whenever it seems like the right thing to do. Let's initiate talks with the French and ask how much we can have straight away. Then a projection of what that leaves us assuming there's a shortfall in terms of number of homes."

"Can I assume that bringing in the military is a good move?" asked Amber. There was general agreement.

"Whatever possessed the staff at Hinkley Point to publish this in a public journal?" mused Theresa.

"I don't think they trusted us politicians to get it right," sighed Boris.

"Leather Jacket Man", or LJM for short, was having a bad time:

- His wife had divorced him and that was a big loss, even though they were still on speaking terms.

- He'd lost his share of the house to the lawyers and the bankers so was in much more modest rented accommodation.

- His declining mental state meant that he was unwilling to socialise or go dating so he was faced with the prospect of being very much on his own.

Furthermore his erratic behaviour had landed him in trouble. After jay-walking on a nature trail on the way in to work one morning, he encountered his meerkat toy in the boardroom and got altogether flustered. He challenged Jack about the situation and Jack rapidly came to the conclusion that LJM was off his rocker.

LJM's mother was called as next of kin and she phoned ahead to emergency services as she knew that the time had come to refer to the NHS.

In the meantime LJM amused himself in the stairwell. He thought that Black Swan Data was all about mining data from the black swans in Dawlish. And relocated the meerkat to the lift seeing as he was officially head of the animal kingdom.

There was no doubting the fact that LJM was in the full grip of psychosis.

When he arrived at A&E he initially cooperated with everything he was asked to do. He was given a triage assessment and then referred to a cubicle. Although he was given some medication to supposedly take the edge off things, it had the opposite effect and sent him loopy.

He was repeatedly going outside the cubicle, interfering with other patients and staff to the extent that the Security Guards were called in. He stood right on the edge of the boundary between the cubicle and the corridor and was pushing in every direction to see when they objected to his behaviour.

After a full assessment, LJM was referred to The Cedars in Exeter for up to one month on a Section 2. He was only able to take the bare minimum of things with him. No sharp objects or anything else that may cause harm. So clothes and a phone basically.

Once in his room, he was made to feel welcome by the staff.

He didn't remember much about the initial few days but he did remember a visit from the consultant psychiatrist Dr Salvi. He brought the news that he'd made a diagnosis and settled on Bipolar Disorder as the most likely thing. He explained that this was consistent with the psychosis that LJM was displaying in A&E.

This meant regular medication with lithium and an anti-psychotic, of which there was a number to choose from. Initially he went with Olanzapine as a good starting point.

Two weeks later, LJM's psychosis proved persistent. By now he was hearing voices as well as imagining strange things. A change to Quetiapine did little to help.

With the combination of everything, LJM buckled under the pressure. In particular his previous experiences whilst being trailed by secret services had gone in very deep and he was struggling to see the difference between fantasy and reality.

For a while he simply paced up and down the corridors and slept in his room. He was not inclined to take part in any of the activities going.

Then after walking as far as he could go countless times in each direction, he'd built up a picture in his mind. He had an artistic idea and wanted to go to Occupational Therapy to do some drawing.

His drawing showed the Eiffel tower in the up and down directions, with the Cedars lodged at the second stage in the north, south, east and west directions. He was taking some artistic licence because the real Cedars is fore-shortened in the west direction. He also took a leap of faith that it could be made stable in mid-air via a cable-stay-bridge style arrangement.

Now in his imaginary 3D mental hospital he could go from nought to infinity in each of the six directions. He drew the background as it would have looked if the structure was located in the middle of Exe Bridges in central Exeter.

The artwork didn't help his mental state and LJM went into a bit of a decline after that. He dreamed he was in a network of rooms connected by round portholes in three dimensions where a massive, interlocked game of Twister was going on. He dreamed that he met a young Albert Einstein in the corridor and that the whole hospital was located in a mine, separated from the rest of the World-War II world. He dreamed that he was working as a surgeon with futuristic technology and that his son was working in the office opposite. Finally he dreamed that he was landing an alien spacecraft using some weird controls in a black-and-white world.

There was an incident where LJM thought that a piece of paper left in the corridor was done deliberately to irritate him. After expressing his concerns, he was rounded upon by six members of staff who did the whole power-and-control thing by bending his wrists back and escorting him off to the detention centre.

After that he hit rock bottom by urinating in the container provided and then spreading it around the inside of the cell. Shortly afterwards, he was transferred to the Psychiatric Intensive Care Unit (PICU) at Kewstoke in neighbouring Somerset.

Julia entered the fray by driving to Hinkley Point. She took the Motorway to Bridgwater, the A39 to Cannington and then a sequence of B roads to Wick, followed by a final approach along Withycombe Hill and Wick Moor Drove.

It was a nice leafy green road which seemed oddly out of place for a nuclear power station. She'd somehow imagined soot-covered walls and smog.

On the way, she'd taken the precaution of booking into the Premier Inn in Bridgwater. Room 202. She was expecting to stay for several days.

When she got to the security barrier she reached inside her coat pocket to extract her ID.

"I'm Julia Barnes, CIA", she said as she waved the badge.

"Thank you miss, the car park is behind us and the main building is over to the left as we look from here," said the Security Guard.

As she went to put her badge back in her pocket, Julia noticed a small yellow label with the number 202 written on it. She didn't remember any encounter with staff at the hotel, so this was completely weird. Almost as if somebody was watching her.

After she'd parked the car and got through reception, she met with the Mongols. She ran to give Henning a hug, shook Theo by the hand and then acted sheepishly in Kingsley's presence. "How are you?" he said.

"I'm doing OK, thanks," she said. "All the better for having a crisis to deal with!"

"Yes it all seems familiar. The whiff of new physics and the prospect of going haring off round the countryside in search of the source," said Henning.

"What have you got so far?" she quizzed.

"We did a circle round the nuclear power plant and it shows a marginally stronger signal on the north-eastern side, basically offshore," said Kingsley.

"So that's the end of the trail?" she asked, visibly disappointed.

"It comes back onshore in Weston-Super-Mare, assuming the signal runs in a straight line," said Theo.

"Doing radiation tests in the grounds of a nuclear power station is one thing. If we start doing them in the middle of a town it will attract all the wrong attention," said Julia.

"Agreed. We need a mobile van as cover. With radiation detectors close to the ground," said Kingsley. "And yes this is all starting to sound familiar!"

Julia phoned back to Q Branch with her requirements. Specifications for the Geiger-Muller tubes close to the ground with computer kit in the back of the van. She was told it would be ready in 24 hours.

So it was back to the hotel and wait. The Mongols were also checked into the Premier Inn so that was easy.

The van arrived next day. "Look after it," said Barney, the driver.

"We will," said Julia.

When they were ready, the four of them took a trip up the M5 and along the A370 to Weston-Super-Mare. They drove into the middle of town along the seafront seeing as they didn't have any better information. After a short while searching, they settled on a parking space next to the beach and seven other sites in a kind of circle around the seafront. One of them would have to be done by holding up the traffic.

Over the course of the next half hour, the van relocated to the eight places. Once the nuclear pulse (NP) measurements were done, the analysis began on the computer.

"The one hertz signal is there. And it's strongest to the north," said Henning.

At this point they were about to head back to base when the police turned up.

"We've had reports of you holding up traffic," said the constable.

"We couldn't get it started," said Henning.

"I expect that's why you were seen getting out of the van and looking underneath."

"Indeed."

"Well go carefully then."

"We will."

They felt like the A-Team in their black Ford transit van.

"We just need the red streak and rear spoiler", joked Julia.

When they got back to the hotel they parked the van and used the bar area as a meeting room.

"So what to make of the north signal?" said Henning.

"The logical thing to do is to look in the Sand Bay area just north of Weston-Super-Mare," said Kingsley.

"There's nothing there unless you count Pontins," said Theo.

"There is a military grade facility in Kewstoke. I've been made aware of it," said Julia.

"And you think this maybe related? This is starting to sound fishy," said Henning.

"What are we doing out here if the military already knows the answer?" demanded Theo.

"Good question," said Kingsley.

"I guess we'd better take a trip to Sand Bay then," replied Julia, boldly.

THE MYSTERY OF KEWSTOKE

Kewstoke Hospital was a lovely old cream Georgian art-deco style building with high ceilings and massive sash windows. Nothing like the Cedars. It took LJM a few days to reorient himself in room seven. Initially he'd been refusing his lithium medication but when he did start to take it again he improved.

Still there was an incident where he was rounded upon by the staff but this time they relocated him to his room and used only minimal force needed to accomplish the task in hand. Because he didn't suffer any torture, he felt that the whole way he was treated was altogether better, even though Kewstoke was supposed to be more of a hell-hole than the Cedars.

In time LJM got better. He did spot a number of inmates who he thought were military spies. One in particular, Will, was an American complete with special forces leather jacket. But on the whole they kept themselves to themselves.

He also had a run-in with Andy the trader. "Nudge, nudge, wink, wink" Andy had said in reference to what was generally going on. LJM was a sucker for that kind of suggestibility and immediately went to trade in his leather jacket for some army trousers, which was a terrible deal.

The way LJM's mind was working, everything had a symbolic value. Even a simple Coke bottle containing water was deemed a fire extinguisher thanks to its red bottle top. Coke Zero was military in black. Another bottle with a bird logo had connections with the seagulls outside.

A particularly persistent seagull woke him up every morning by pecking on the window until he opened the sash, at which point it would fly away. He put some digestive biscuits out on the ledge but food seemed to be a secondary thing.

Then there was an Animal hoodie in green. Barter traded. Nature again.

And a sequence of Kill-Star T-shirts in black: Giza, Vulture, Weed-Be-Out-There and Space-Grass.

He wanted to set fire to a ten pound note, such was the strength of his feelings. He was still clearly unwell.

At this point he was detained on a Section 3, up to six months. However, the timescale was reviewed before the allotted time was up and was extended if deemed necessary. So it was a rolling six months; he could get stuck there forever.

Part way through his stay, LJM was given the opportunity to have some town leave. It had to be escorted so a member of staff, Barbara, took the taxi with him. It was a short trip into the town centre in Weston-Super-Mare.

He wanted to buy a book, which was a sensible choice for being stuck in hospital, so they went to Waterstones first. Then to Costa for a coffee. Then the sci-fi memorabilia shop and finally Little Witch where he bought a Merkaba star made of red jasper.

When it came to catching a cab for the ride back, LJM was caught between stools. On the one hand he wanted to cooperate. On the other hand he felt drawn to the silver sculpture / tower / thing and wanted to resist. In the event he didn't wander very far from Barbara but it was enough for her to sense what was going on.

When they got back to base, she reported that psychosis was still very much in evidence. Which meant he had to explain it to the doctor at the next weekly ward-round.

He sort-of did this this by explaining what was going on in his head and then taking strides around the meeting room, finally sitting in the corner. "I see," said Doctor Barker. So his stay continued…

LJM invested his time wisely:

- On the one hand, he was inclined to read and was recommended "Be Here Now" by R.Dass of the Lama Foundation. So he got hold of it via Waterstones in Weston-Super-Mare.

- On the other hand, he was also inclined to write and started two books, one a true story based on his own experiences and the other a fictional story with a number of truths woven in. He wrote in freehand and sent it in weekly packets to his mother who was a trained typist.

After she reported their results from Weston-Super-Mare, Julia was put on hold. When the caller eventually got back he said "Visit the military base at Kewstoke, northern Weston-Super-Mare".

Julia went pale.

"Are you saying that you've known all along what the source of this thing is but you've kept it from me and my team?" she demanded.

"Let's just say we're one step ahead of you for a change," he replied.

"Can I take my team with me?" she asked.

"Yes," came the reply.

Julia agreed to go.

She got in the van with the other three. She already knew most of the way there from Bridgwater, it was just a minor change to take the B3440, Queen's way and then Church Road.

"So what do you know about Kewstoke?" asked Henning.

"That's classified," said Julia. "They'll make you sign the Official Secrets Act."

When they got to the main gate, two soldiers were waiting.

"Please state your business," asserted the first soldier.

"Julia Barnes, CIA".

"I'll check your clearance," said the second soldier.

After a while he came back with "Access denied. So Julia got on the phone.

"We should have access for three males and myself," she exclaimed.

"Yes that's fine miss."

"I wonder if they'll let us drive on their lawn?" mused Kingsley.

"One way to find out."

The soldiers turned a blind eye ...

They travelled up the main drive and parked in the staff car park, admiring the vast building and grounds.

When they got to reception, another couple of soldiers were waiting. They let Julia in through the main door operated by key-card with an internal release; this was quite clearly a secure operation. The other three had to wait their turn to sign the Official Secrets Act before they would be let in through the door.

Julia was escorted upstairs to Sandford Ward.

"Is this a hospital? I thought it was supposed to be a military base," she asked.

"It was a hospital. Now it's military," came the reply. "I'm Delia by the way".

Once they'd got past the heavy door they walked along the corridor to an open door.

"Please come inside," said Delia.

Julia cooperated. "What is this?" she gestured towards the large machine in the middle of the room.

"This is the thought machine (TM)," Delia replied. "Try it for yourself". She gestured towards a set of headphones.

Julia accepted the invitation. "What thoughts?"

"A targeted individual."

"No way. In this room?"

"No it's not any of us in here. You don't need to know exactly who."

At this point she was joined by Theo, Henning and Kingsley.

Julia listened intently. There were seemingly random background noises along with specific voices and a machine-generated sub-vocalisation.

"The sub-vocalisation is the clever part. It was relatively easy to get the technology to hear the other voices," said Delia. "Having done that it's then a logical step to hook up the thoughts to a database and build up a picture of what the individual is likely to come up with next.

"This is outrageous. I take it the individual concerned has no idea he or she is being monitored?"

"It's completely non-invasive".

"But also completely unethical".

Silence.

When it was time for his monthly medical, LJM went down to the medication room. They measured his height and weight and blood pressure.

"Your pulse is 56 beats per minute".

The remaining tests were all normal so he was given the all-clear.

At his next ward round, LJM was informed that he would be transferred back to Devon. There was a hold-up at The Cedars due to a bed situation but he would be sent to one of the other hospitals instead.

Within a few days he was out of PICU and back into Open Acute, albeit in a different town.

GO OVER IT
AGAIN

The politicians finally took the decision to pull the plug on Hinkley Point. The arrangements had been made to cover with extra power from the French so there was no argument to the contrary.

In the control room the necessary switches were pulled to initiate the shutdown sequence. Once complete an engineer called out "We're offline". After which there was a deathly silence.

The Mongols were in the power station laboratory where the initial one hertz detection was made.

"Any effect?" asked Henning, hopefully.

"No the signal's still there," came the reply. "Weaker but still there".

"So we can eliminate power generation as the source," said Theo. "We already knew that".

"We should remeasure outside," asserted Kingsley.

Once they'd redone the circle of measurements outside, there was a change. Whereas the original signal was to the east and offshore, it was now to the west and onshore. They agreed that the strength of the signal was weaker.

"What to make of that? A 180 degree shift," said Kingsley.

"We never did do the measurements in Kewstoke. How about we do that first to see what the situation is?" said Henning.

"Agreed."

So it was back in the van for another trip to Kewstoke, this time with the freedom outdoors rather than the controlled circumstances offered by the military.

They spent half an hour doing measurements in a circle as before.

Then analysed the results and came to the conclusion that the signal was all but gone, with a weak indicator south-west.

"They've changed something," concluded Theo. "If we'd done this a day earlier I bet we'd have caught whatever they were doing in that hospital."

"It's hard to know without more information. If the TM was the source then maybe they've just moved it to another facility. If it was a geographical signal then it's changed somehow for reasons unclear. If it was a biological signal then maybe the targeted individual has moved on and taken the game elsewhere," postulated Henning.

"Julia, can you phone for more information?" asked Kingsley.

Julia agreed.

After she was on the phone for ten minutes, she put down the handset and addressed the others.

"In a nutshell, they confirm that the signal is biological in origin. The individual concerned was in Kewstoke but has now been moved. They won't say where," she stated.

"What about the thought machine?" asked Henning.

"It isn't thought to be relevant," joked Julia, noticing her own pun.

"So what next?" asked Kingsley.

"We head back to Hinkley Point and make one last set of measurements before we head off across the countryside," replied Julia.

"Anyone would think we're chasing LJM again," said Theo.

"In that case I bet we'll end up in Exeter," said Henning.

"Second that," said Kingsley.

By the time they got back to Hinkley Point, a brand-new military cordon was in place.

Barbed wire had gone up and the entrance was now at the end of Wick Moor Drove. Effectively they were giving the nuclear power station a wider berth even though it was now switched off. Similar precautions were being taken around every other nuclear power plant around the country.

The state of alarm in the press was palpable. They were calling for the closure of all nuclear power stations even though Hinkley Point was the only one that found the one hertz signal.

The protestors were still out in force. The fact that Hinkley Point had been switched off was of no reassurance to them. They still feared a runaway explosion and wanted more to be done to contain the blast.

"BURY HP IN CONCRETE" read the placard.

When the van made it through the cordon, they parked it and set up their portable experiment. Half an hour later they were chewing on the results.

"Same as before," said Theo.

"That's reassuring," said Kingsley.

Is it worth getting a more precise fix on direction before we go anywhere else? We could put points in between points," said Henning.

They all agreed and spent another half an hour refining their results.

"North Devon" was the best they could come up with.

"Could still be Exeter" was an observation based on the uncertainty of the results.

Julia decided she would give it a miss for the predictable trip across country the next day. She offered Theo a day off on the basis that Henning and Kingsley could cover the van operations. Shopping in Bridgwater for him then.

"Julia, assuming this information is correct and the signal is biological in origin, then presumably we're going to bump into him or her if we keep going at it well enough. Then what? Keeping clear of any nuclear power stations would seem to be a good bet. Likewise for any nuclear missile sites or submarines. Avoiding Plymouth then as well as Hinkley point. Perhaps we should find somewhere half way in between the two?" reasoned Theo.

"That sounds reasonable but it will all get political before then. We can't keep someone confined at gunpoint without resorting to terrorist legislation, which is hardly warranted for someone in hospital."

"What kind of hospital is Kewstoke?" asked Henning.

"It's actually a private Cygnet mental hospital, I looked it up" said Julia. "The military veneer is just a ruse."

"In that case the individual concerned has either been released or transferred to another mental hospital. Do we know what ward they were on?" said Henning.

"Sandford Ward is an Open Acute but was apparently empty of real patients while the military were doing their thing with the TM" said Kingsley.

"Nash Ward is downstairs and is a PICU. If the targeted individual wasn't in Sandford then presumably the room below was the most likely location. In which case we're looking at a transfer to Open Acute elsewhere" said Theo.

"There is an Open Acute in Exeter, Torbay, Plymouth or Barnstaple. That's it for Devon," said Julia.

"In which case driving straight to Barnstaple, given that it's in North Devon, then doing a test in the hospital car park is the way to go," announced Kingsley.

Julia could see that she wasn't going to get her day off after all.

OCEAN VIEW IN BARNSTAPLE

The next day they all drove in the van from Bridgwater, down the M5 to junction 27 then along the North Devon Link Road to Barnstaple.

When they arrived at the main hospital car park, they asked directions for the mental hospital and were told that Ocean View ward was at the end of the right turn, follow it round to the left.

There was nowhere obvious to do a set of van measurements, so they elected to do portable tests on the grass instead.

The results confirmed what they already suspected.

"The targeted individual is most likely in Ocean View ward. We have a strong signal all round with direction," summarised Henning.

Julia got on the phone immediately. "I know you wanted to keep us in the dark but we're currently stood in the car park of Barnstaple hospital. Do we get the prize?" she demanded.

There was a long pause.

"Correct. But we need more time to clear some other patients out of the way and make room for the military."

"So you're going for the same setup as at Kewstoke? Why the move? You could have just left him there," retorted Julia.

"He was too close to Hinkley Point," came the answer.

Julia smiled to herself at the confirmation that the targeted individual is a *he*. "When are you going to tell me this is LJM we're chasing?"

Another long pause.

"You seem to know it all, Miss Barnes."

"When will the TM be in place, assuming that's what you're up to?

"Give us three days."

"In the meantime I'd like to set up permanent monitoring around Ocean View ward. Geiger Muller tubes as before, in protective housing with cables running inside the building. Eight of them. Then desktop computer apparatus to crunch the results. If you can't do inside the building then we'll have to make do with the van," she commanded.

"We'll also need kit set up permanently inside. Ideally inside his room and at common locations in the ward such as the kitchen or sitting area," added Theo.

"What will happen to LJM?" asked Henning.

"He'll either be released or held indefinitely. We can work out the paperwork either way," was the answer.

"Released?" queried Kingsley.

"There is a growing swell of support for him that are saying none of this is his fault so he should just be set free and we take it from there."

"Fat chance of that," snorted Henning. "I know how these political situations work."

When they were done with their questions, Julia hung up. "Finally I get my day off," she said.

The organisation was as good as its word. Three days later access was granted to the corridor outside Ocean View ward where the requested kit had been assembled.

With the detectors permanently set up, they could analyse for much longer periods of time and get more accurate results.

Initially they could see no deviation in the signals which were placed symmetrically in a circle surrounding the ward. Then it gradually became clear that they could track where LJM was in the ward.

"That's a result," said Theo.

"I wonder where they've put the TM?" mused Henning. "It's grass on three sides of the ward and the near end simply opens onto this corridor. The only place to hide would be in a room in the ward itself."

"I'll ask them the next time I phone in," said Julia.

Donald Trump got on the phone to Theresa May.

"I hear that your main man has landed himself in more trouble," he said.

"Nothing we can't handle," she replied.

"Oh come on. The political hot potato who was at the centre of your last fiasco now finds himself in the same situation. At least he's in mental hospital this time. You're not proposing to set him free any time soon are you?" he continued.

"That depends on the clinical judgement of the doctors concerned. Once the section expires, he's a free man; he's done nothing wrong at the end of the day," she said, delighting in her semicolon.

"He should be locked up in a secure scientific environment. That's the be-all-and-end-all of it. We can offer him a salary and give him the usual two weeks leave but he won't have any real freedom. This is an inevitable consequence of being the source of new physics," Donald reasoned.

"Well we'll have to differ on that. He's not a fossil or a lab rat. You can't dig him up and dissect him. He's a live human being," huffed Theresa.

"I still don't see what the problem is. We'll offer him a dream job at an astronomical salary so he can't say no," insisted Donald.

"It's a matter of principle."

"That was fine when he was a passive end-point on a signal, but now he's an active controller of the timing of nuclear decay events. That's entirely different."

"If you say so," she sighed.

Julia was informed by Linda, a member of hospital staff that the patient known as "LJM" was being granted town leave.

"Whereabouts is he going?"

"I don't know, you'll have to ask him. Probably down the High Street and back again. He's only got an hour," said Linda.

Julia considered the situation. "Is the High Street" pedestrianised?"

"No".

In Julia's mind that meant she could take the van. With two of them on foot they could cover all angles.

"Are you sure you want to do this?" asked Kingsley. "This is his private time. Nobody's ordering us to tail him."

"We might not get another opportunity like this. If we get just one measurement it will be worth it" replied Julia.

Henning and Theo agreed to follow on foot but wanted to alert LJM that they would be there so as not to alarm him.

Julia asked Linda if she could warn LJM and she agreed.

When he set off through the doors of Ocean View ward, LJM recognised them all. Then Julia and Kingsley went ahead in the van and waited at the end of the High Street, which would be 15 minutes' walk from the hospital.

LJM had encountered the CIA before so he wasn't particularly concerned. He decided to focus on his walk and ignore the fact that they were following.

"This is weird. We can't introduce ourselves or we're breaking the Official Secrets Act," said Henning.

"No doubt Julia and Kingsley will think of something. It's an ideal chance to get LJM in the van and take some real close-up measurements. We could give him a lift back so he doesn't go over on his time," replied Theo.

LJM meanwhile completed his walk as far as High Street, where the van was waiting. He took no notice and the van followed.

Kingsley managed to take a measurement as they were moving along. Then LJM took a right turn down a pedestrianised street. Henning and Theo followed on foot, until he got to the end and turned left.

"It looks like he's going to the library," said Henning.

When the van caught up, they managed to take another reading outside the library before LJM emerged with a book he'd purchased.

This was the critical moment.

"Sir" called Kingsley.

"Yes".

"We can give you a lift back to the hospital in return for your cooperation."

"Cooperation with what?"

"We'd like to make some measurements. Completely safe and non-invasive".

LJM thought about it for a while.

"OK."

They decided to keep the van in situ while LJM sat on the back seat. Kingsley placed one Geiger Muller tube near his forehead and Henning placed another near his chest.

"What are you doing?" asked LJM.

"That's classified," said Julia.

They quickly deduced that his heart was giving the stronger signal. However, with no way of measuring his pulse they wouldn't be able to correlate his heartbeat until more sophisticated test equipment was put together.

At this point the army turned up in a Foxhound military vehicle from the war in Afghanistan.

They didn't appear to have any specific orders regarding LJM but they were very clear that the territory in the corridor outside Ocean View now belonged to them. So the Mongols had to remove their kit.

"We've just gone to the trouble of putting this together and now you're tearing it down," complained Kingsley.

"From now on only military hardware will be used in this operation," came the curt reply.

"You're standing in the way of scientific progress," said Henning.

"You'll need a combined heartrate monitor and Geiger-Muller tube to make the next step," said Theo, to deaf ears.

"And what has happened to your thought machine? We never did hear back on that score," said Julia.

Julia phoned base and confirmed that they were effectively out of a job. So they put their kit in the van, climbed in and drove back to Bristol Airport. Kinglsey, Henning and Theo took flights from there while Julia agreed to take the van back to base.

LJM was confused. He noted that the CIA were no longer there when he next took leave; and clearly that they had been replaced by a heavy British Army presence.

Then when he got to the car park he could see the American Army in a camouflaged Hummer military vehicle. He was made to turn back.

In his mildly psychotic state, his thoughts were running riot. He'd never quite believed the sequence of things that happened up until this point but now there was no denying that things were real.

When he got back inside and asked about the leave situation, he was told that he would have to wait until they got back to him.

"But I am clinically well enough to have the leave. The system is the system. What's the problem," he complained loudly.

That night LJM slept up until the sound of breaking glass woke him at midnight. It was difficult to see in the dark but he could make out two figures dressed in black in the hallway. They indicated in broken English that he was to follow them through the window at the far end. With guns. Otherwise LJM wouldn't have gone with them.

Amazingly the British and American armies were on the other side of the building and had not provided complete coverage on their patrols. In their minds, the fact that it was a secure ward caused them to be off their guard when it came to a break-in. They didn't even hear it because the bandits used a cloth to muffle the sounds.

They ran across the grass and through the trees to a car waiting on the main road, next to the bus stop. This bypassed all the military presence in the car park and evaded the next patrol round the perimeter.

There was quite an uproar within the military as to how this could have happened. Having said that, this was a first for the NHS, to have a patient broken out of mental hospital by terrorist attack.

Theresa May phoned Donald Trump to give him the bad news.

"It seems we've been the target of a terrorist operation to break LJM out from the care of the NHS," she said.

"What?? This man is way too valuable to risk him like that," he exclaimed.

"I'm assured by my technical advisers that we can track him anyway so they shouldn't get far," said Theresa coolly.

With that the Mongols were called in once again with Julia at the helm. The military were under instructions to follow and assist where they could.

"We don't need that kind of attention," complained Henning.

"We're under orders," stated Julia. "Plain and simple."

"If they keep moving then we'll never find him," said Kingsley. "The resolution on our measurements is simply too vague. We got lucky with Barnstaple by thinking it through given known information. We need intelligence of some kind to stand a chance in this situation".

"OK, well what do you propose? Make it a problem for the military, or kick it upstairs?" mused Henning.

"Julia, I concur with Kingsley and Henning. We need more information and we don't have the resources ourselves to get it," summarised Theo.

"I'll take it from here," said Julia.

Julia spoke to her contacts in the British and American armies. "We simply don't know where he's gone," she said. "Whatever help you can provide will be essential".

"Your best bet will be MI5", said the American.

"Agreed", said the British. "We don't have this on a military radar."

Julia was faced with the prospect of approaching MI5 directly, given her status as CIA, or phone upstairs and get them to do it. She elected to contact MI5 directly.

"Giles, it's Julia Barnes from the CIA" she said to the phone.

"Julia it's good to hear from you. How can I help?"

"We have an intractable situation with the loss of LJM from under the military noses. They claim they don't have any intel on where he is either. Almost makes you think they're being deliberately useless."

"And you want us to find him for you?"

"Surely you have more than enough reason to want to find him yourselves given what we now know".

"Which is what?"

"That he's the source of synchronised radioactive decay events as reported by Hinkley Point. LJM was in Kewstoke at the time, which corresponds to the north-east signal we found on the ground. We've established a stronger signal the nearer we've got to him."

Julia took a call from Theresa May.

"I hear that you've tracked the source of this radioactive situation to the man already known to us as LJM", opened Theresa.

"Yes that's correct. We were following a signal from Hinkley Point to Kewstoke just north of Weston-Super-Mare and then to Barstaple where we lost him to terrorist intervention," replied Julia.

"Do you have any idea where he is?" asked Theresa.

"We've yet to start tracking him. Our success so far has been based on additional intelligence as to his location in mental hospital. Now I assume he's out in the wider world he could be anywhere and we get only an approximate direction from the signal detection experiment. I was hoping you could provide me with additional intelligence from MI5 as to where he's likely to be given who's involved," responded Julia.

"I don't have any information to pass on. I'll brief MI5 as to the situation and hand it over to them. They should keep you in the loop," said Theresa.

"I was just on the phone to them before your call," observed Julia.

"I think that concludes it then. Finding LJM is top priority and I leave you in the capable hands of MI5".

Julia returned with the Mongols to Barnstaple.

"Is there any way we can build improved kit with better resolution?" she asked.

"There are lots of options. For starters we could build a parallel machine with multiple detectors so we can measure simultaneously. If we incorporate 16 detectors then that will double our resolution compared to the laborious approach we've taken so far," proposed Kingsley.

"We could also improve resolution by triangulating in any given location. Our increased measuring speed will make this viable," added Henning.

"Spend a few days working up a detailed proposal. Then we can see what's involved and how to go about implementing it. I think it's worthwhile to aim at the best measurements we can and take slightly longer about it rather than rushing in with incremental changes," she commanded.

"Back to the hotel then", said Kingsley.

"Will we have a base of operations on this job?" asked Henning.

"Surely the unpredictable whereabouts of LJM makes that unlikely," responded Theo.

"Perhaps we could at least visit the people who will making it?" asked Henning.

"Yes that's a good idea," said Julia. "We can visit London".

"Let's do the Natural History Museum in the same trip," added Theo, sarcastically.

HIDING IN PLAIN SIGHT

L JM quickly made up his mind to escape from the company of the terrorists he was with. Using his penchant for ad-lib he simply walked out unnoticed. He then took the train to Exeter.

He knew that the CIA would follow him to the ends of the earth so there was little point in running. Also he only had limited funds so there was a limit to how much time he could spend in a foreign country even if he wanted to,

He decided that the best policy was to hide, so he did the unthinkable; he took off his leather jacket. Now LJM became No Leather Jacket Man.

Also he didn't want to go back to his flat in Exeter because he knew they would be watching so he elected to become homeless instead.

Then LJM had a panicky moment. What if the thought machine was still monitoring his thoughts? He was aware of the TM as a concept in his mind. What he didn't know was the extent to which it had been implemented for real in Kewstoke. Perhaps LJM had become aware at the same time as they implemented it.

Did reality create thought or did thought create reality?

What kind of universe did he want to live in? Did he have a choice? Or was it just coincidence?

"The first place to search for LJM has got to be Exeter," said Julia. "That's his home."

"I think you'll find him wandering the streets," said Theo.

"What makes you say that?" asked Julia.

"Just a hunch. That's what I would do to escape terrorists and evade detection."

"There is one more option," added Kingsley. "We don't know what the range on the thought machine is. I'd put money on the idea that LJM was the target individual we heard being monitored in Kewstoke. If it extends out into the wider world … how far? Does it reach Exeter? Or does it have to be located in the same town?"

"I doubt they'd give you that level of information, being classified as it is," said Henning.

"It makes you think though. Can they monitor all of us, or does it have to be a special kind of individual? Is the thought process two-way so that the targeted individual is aware of things known to the TM?" continued Kingsley.

"OK I get the message. I'll see if I can put some pressure on the military to answer our questions," accepted Julia.

<hr>

Julia came back with another invitation to Kewstoke.

"So clearly they haven't relocated it just yet," she observed.

"Let's go," said Kingsley, speaking for all of them.

When they arrived at Kewstoke, they all bundled into the TM room with Delia.

"Delia, can you give yes / no answers to the following questions please?" asked Julia.

"I'll do my best," replied Delia.

"Is Leather Jack Man or LJM the targeted individual?"

"He was but he subsequently left the hospital downstairs."

"Does the range on the TM extend to Exeter?"

"He's currently out of range so assuming he's in Exeter then that's a no."

"Does the range extend to Weston-Super-Mare?"

"We tracked him while he was on town leave. So that's a yes."

"Is the TM relocatable?"

"With some considerable effort, yes."

"Would you be prepared to relocate it to Exeter so we can use it to track down LJM?"

"I'd have to put in a request to that effect. What guarantee do we have that he's actually there?" asked Delia.

"This is just a working theory at this stage," replied Julia. "It's his home."

"Well he's the only individual known to work with the TM. So he's very valuable to us. I'd expect they'd sign off on that," elaborated Delia.

"How did you find him then?" asked Julia.

"We were on a bit of a long shot monitoring patients in Kewstoke and he just walked right in," responded Delia.

"Fate," observed Julia.

Whether it was fate or not that LJM encountered the thought machine in Kewstoke, it was equally likely to be fate that the thought machine would encounter LJM in Exeter. The military signed off on relocating it temporarily and rented a room in the Phoenix Centre in the middle of Exeter. They were serious about hanging on to their only targeted individual.

With Delia at the helm the TM was set up in record time and she switched it on ready to listen.

Almost instantly she could hear the familiar sounds and thoughts that were LJM's. However, what she could not do was project any thoughts back to him. This was one-way communication only.

"Julia, it's Delia. I've got a fix on LJM. He's somewhere in Exeter, I'd say."

"When it comes down to it, that's not overly helpful. We could do with a more accurate fix than that," replied Julia.

"I'm afraid I can't be more specific than that. The best I can do is to monitor his thoughts in case he comes out with something useful," ruled Delia.

"Right you are," acknowledged Julia.

She put the phone down.

"Well, boys, we're back to tracking LJM by nuclear pulse. The TM has told us that he's located somewhere in Exeter, but subject to ongoing thought monitoring, that's all," announced Julia.

"How about we do the first measurement at the Phoenix Centre seeing as that's from where the TM is listening," said Kingsley.

"Agreed," said Henning.

They drove to the location in Gandy Street opposite the Phoenix and deployed the latest 16-way NP device. It was just as well they had a result within five minutes seeing as they were blocking the street. The result gave them a direction of the riverside.

They then decided to park the van in the Cathedral and City car park and walk down to the riverside to watch out for LJM.

It didn't take long. Theo spotted him as he came out of Samuel Jones, even without his leather jacket.

"How did you find me?" quizzed LJM.

"It wasn't difficult really. We had some automated assistance," admitted Theo.

"Julia, it's Theo. I have LJM in my sights."

"Is he cooperating?" asked Julia.

"Yes he seems to be," observed Theo.

"Well if you could gently suggest to him that he comes with us, that would be great," suggested Julia.

Julia relayed the call to Giles.

"Giles, we have LJM in our care. But we have no remit to detain him. Can you advise?"

"So where is he" asked Giles.

"In central Exeter," replied Julia.

"Did you get him with the thought machine?"

"Partly. We also used a nuclear pulse measurement."

"How did you even know which town to look in?"

"Call it a hunch."

"Well I'll send the police to detain him. On charges of breaching the peace."

Sure enough a police car turned up five minutes later, to escort LJM off to Heavitree Police Station.

"This is bullshit. I haven't breached any peace," moaned LJM.

"If you set off Hinkley Point that will be more than enough peace shattered to last a lifetime."

"But I haven't done anything. You can't arrest me because of what might happen," complained LJM.

"Actually we can arrest you under terrorism laws. We have fairly broad powers to detain suspected terrorists".

"But I have no intention of being a terrorist. Anything that happens is by accident."

"Hmmm. Sounds like a recipe for a dangerous situation."

"Actually we have the option of using the thought machine to tell if he's a terrorist or not," postulated Theo.

"And you are who, exactly?" queried the police officer.

Theo went quiet.

"Well, welll, well. Three holes in the ground. You're free to go while we escort Bob here to the police station."

By this time Henning and Kingsley had caught up with Theo just in time to see LJM carted off.

"We should alert Delia to this situation. That LJM is accused of being a terrorist," insisted Theo.

"Relax, mate. I'm sure LJM isn't going anywhere," advised Kingsley.

NEAR DEATH EXPERIENCE

The duty sergeant was having a hard time understanding the charges against LJM. At one level they seemed so preposterous as to be almost farcical. At another level they seemed so deadly serious it would be a massive mistake to have this man on the loose. He elected to take the safe approach and contacted the Crown Prosecution Service. Within a couple of hours the CPS came back with the decision to detain him in Maximum Security pending trial.

So LJM was taken to Dartmoor Prison in Princetown, 20 miles north of Plymouth.

Almost immediately, the monitors on a nuclear submarine stationed at Devonport Dockyard picked up the one hertz signal.

"Sir, it's not ubiquitous but it's definitely there," reported the signals operator.

"So Hinkley Point were right after all," concluded the captain.

The matter rapidly landed on the prime minister's desk, with recommendations from all and sundry.

The Royal Navy were seeing it as a curiosity, not a major cause for alarm. Admittedly they were unaware of the whereabouts of LJM.

The scientific adviser was in agreement. If they could reproduce the results just by relocating LJM then the threat seemed a whole lot less imminent than it did at Hinkley Point.

The home secretary was still alarmed.

The foreign secretary was told it was none of his business.

Theresa May took the decision that come what may, none of this was LJM's fault so he should be released immediately. With his cooperation, he would carry a tracking device at all times, implanted in his skull. This way they would always know his whereabouts for the purpose of monitoring nuclear power stations and submarines.

Julia and the Mongols decided to regroup following the prime minister's decision. Effectively it ended the manhunt that was the search for the origin of the nuclear pulse signal. It freed them up from continually doing more tests and made them available to consider the science from a wider viewpoint.

The military decided to put in a bid for LJM's time considering he was so valuable to them in thought machine terms. As he was out of mental hospital this was a good time.

LJM agreed to both the operation to implant a tracking device and to the military's offer to spend time with them. They would sort out security so that he didn't face an immediate risk of another terrorist kidnap.

LJM was recovering from his operation in Exeter Wonford hospital when general Harry Piers came to see him.

"Son, you've had a busy week. You're lucky to be all in one piece," he said.

"Ben? Ben Kenobi? Boy am I glad to see you," said LJM, quoting Star Wars.

Harry smiled.

"What can I do for you, general?"

"I just wanted to say how crucial you are in advancing the state of the art. Your decision to join us is a bonus for us all. Your work with the thought machine is instrumental and your work with nuclear pulse signals is fundamental. Thank goodness the terrorists didn't get to hang on to you for long," posited Harry.

"I guess that makes the tracking device all the more relevant. I could do with a briefing on what this thought machine actually is. I have a vague idea but it's probably wrong. And nobody has explained what nuclear pulse is all about," responded LJM.

"I'll arrange for you to visit Delia who is the TM operator. And I'll arrange for the Mongols to visit for a general briefing," offered Harry.

"The Mongols?"

"Julia Barnes, Kingsley Khan, Henning Horlicks and Theofanes Raptor."

"All good," agreed LJM.

In the first instance, LJM visited the Phoenix Centre for a session with Delia and the TM.

"Hello Bob, I'm Delia."

"Please to meet you, Delia," greeted LJM.

"The object of interest is this machine, here in the centre of the room. This is the thought machine (TM). We have no idea why it targets you as an individual, but ever since you set foot in Kewstoke we've been aware that yours is the signal it's tracking."

"So that's what was going on. I had a vague notion of being monitored but I had no idea it was this blatant."

"Yes, we were in the room upstairs as it turned out. We were experimenting on mental health patients in general, until you turned up".

"So is it the fact that I'm a mental health patient that gives me this status?"

"We have no idea. It seems unlikely to be a coincidence."

"Can I have a go?"

"Sure if you pick up these headphones…" she started to say "… hang on, is this such a good idea? Will it setup a feedback loop in your brain?"

LJM shrugged and picked up the headphones anyway. The sensation was one of listening to his inner voice.

"That's not painful at all," he declared, much to Delia's relief.

Then he noticed that he was getting hotter. Rapidly hotter. And with that his head dripped sweat all over the TM.

"I'm not feeling well," he declared, and fled the TM room for good.

MI5 were put in charge of the thought machine project and Julia and the Mongols transferred their allegiance from the CIA to them. The immediate priority was rollout to every city in the UK so they could look for other targeted individuals.

The manufacture of the TMs was still under military control. And the operators would be military trained.

Given the scale of the operation, it attracted attention from overseas. All of a sudden everyone wanted a thought machine to see if there were any targeted individuals in their country.

So MI6 effectively took control away from MI5 and became the priority customers for the initial round of manufacture.

To cut a long story short, they didn't find anything. All the big cities in the world came back as negative for targeted individuals. So control was passed to Julia and her team to think the problem through.

"If you think back to the Blue Crystal operation the electromagnetic (EM) machine showed positive results at Exeter and. Alice Springs. Exeter turned out to be LJM and Alice Springs turned out to be Patsy. I'd put money on Patsy being another targeted individual," announced Kingsley.

"What about in Exeter? There was another weak signal?" queried Theo.

"Yes there was a minor signal in the direction of Crediton," agreed Henning.

"That gives us two places to follow through with the TM. Thank you," accepted Julia.

For the Crediton operation, they had to rent a room as there was no practical way of getting the TM into even a Ford Luton van. Delia was particular about the quiet surroundings needed so no way was she going to accept being out in the street. This was all assuming that the Phoenix Centre in Exeter was out of range for a Crediton measurement, which seemed to be the case.

When it was operational, the initial results were discouraging. Nobody within range. But Delia left it running into the evening and success. There was a targeted individual somewhere in Crediton. And from the stream of thoughts, something about 'homework' was the order of the day.

MI6 turned the problem over to MI5 to identify who it was. A computer based search revealed that LJM's youngest daughter Esther was the most likely candidate.

It was decided to keep the TM in place in Crediton and to introduce a TM in Torquay where Esther went to school. Furthermore they sent a nuclear submarine from Plymouth to Torquay harbour to see if the nuclear pulse effect was repeated.

At no point did anyone stop to think whether it was appropriate for MI5 and the Royal Navy to be stalking a teenager in this way.

Esther herself was oblivious to what was going on. Whereas her father, LJM, had a vision of a thought machine monitoring his thoughts, Esther was troubled by no such imagining.

Another line of investigation was for Esther's brother Alex and her sister Harriet. If it ran in the family then surely they would be just as likely to have picked it up. Alex was at Nottingham university and Harriet was at Southampton university. The decision was taken to place a TM at each of these locations. Delia supervised by visiting each of them in turn and listening to their thoughts.

Alex's take-away thought was 'football'.

Harriet's take-away thought was 'kayacking'.

Delia was delighted to have three targeted individuals to listen to rather than just one. "So there is an upside to losing LJM," she thought.

At least Alex and Harriet were adults so the stalking didn't seem so entirely inappropriate as it did with Esther.

Giles called a meeting with Julia and the Mongols in Thames House in London.

"The main piece of news is that all three of LJM's children pass the thought machine test and so far Esther has passed the nuclear pulse test as well. We have every reason to believe that Alex and Harriet will too we just need to park a nuclear submarine in Southampton docks. A little more difficult to so that with Nottingham," he said.

"Are we actually going to contact any of the three children like we do with LJM?" asked Henning.

"That depends on the political pressure to do so," advised Giles. "We've taken the decision to stay at arm's length for now. We can see what the TM brings up in each case."

"What about my suggestion that Patsy should be a targeted individual?" queried Kingsley.

"Thus far we've been unable to contact her," said Giles.

"I can find her, assuming she's still in Alice Springs," said Kingsley.

"What will you do, use your EM machine?" asked Giles.

"Yes."

"Off you go to Australia then. I expect to see you back here with Patsy."

Kingsley went back home to Sydney and dusted off his EM machine in the form of SuperCamper. This was a left-over from the Blue Crystal operation, complete will tank of conducting gel in the back in the garage area.

He drove it to Alice Springs which entailed a long trip across the outback. He drove straight into the centre of town to the last known location of Patsy, albeit 3 years previously. He realised this was a bit of a long shot, but he deployed the EM machine and took a measurement of the signal in the surrounding area.

He was expecting a large geographic signal in the direction of EM south, but was hoping for a minor signal in the direction of Patsy.

He was disappointed. Patsy had clearly moved on and simply wasn't there. With no indication from the signal as to where to look, this was a dead end.

Kingsley went back to Giles empty-handed. "Can't we do a search for all people named Patsy? We never did know her surname."

"The list will be too long to follow up on," said Giles.

"What about we repeat the steps that led us to her in the first place?" asked Henning.

"You mean with LJM's assistance," said Theo. "I'm not sure even he knows how he did it."

"Well we can ask," said Giles. He got out his phone and dialled LJM.

"LJM? It's Giles. We have an assignment for you. We need you to get in contact with Patsy again. She is suspected as being the other known targeted individual. This is vitally important for the health of the program that we find everyone out there who is compatible with the thought machine."

LJM agreed that he would start the hunt for Patsy.

"How on earth do I go about this?" he muttered to himself.

The first order of the day was to initiate a telepathy call to see if he could contact her directly. He threw himself down on the ground in central Exeter on the off-chance that it would work.

It didn't.

The second order of the day was to retrace his steps to Topsham, where he had seen the old blind seal on the riverbank all those years ago. And where he had been the last time when he had contacted Patsy this way.

An hour later he was spread-eagled on the ground on the riverbank and still nothing. Either he had lost his touch or Patsy wasn't listening.

He then did something even more unusual. He went hunting in the contacts one his phone to see if by some chance he had stored Patsy in there.

Success!

He phoned it but the number was disconnected.

Nevertheless, not to be put off, he phoned Giles and gave him the number.

Giles immediately went on the system and traced the number to Patsy Valerian.

"Bingo" he shouted.

He went on to trace Patsy Valerian through the rest of the system and got current address and phone details.

He gave the corrected phone number to LJM.

LJM then phoned Patsy for the fourth time that afternoon and finally got through.

"Patsy? It's Bob. I realise it's been three years but how are you?" he asked.

"Bob, my world has changed. I'm a married woman with two young children," she responded.

"So no chance of you heading off to the UK for a bit of scientific research?" he asked, hopefully.

"No, a frayed knot," she replied, metaphorically.

LJM reported back to Giles.

Giles then put it to the Mongols. "We have Patsy's contact details, but she isn't relocatable. The obvious thing to do is to send the TM to Australia. Any thoughts?"

"We could go back in the with the EM machine," said Kingsley.

"And the QE machine too," said Henning.

"Won't Patsy think we're ganging up on her?" quizzed Theo.

"That depends on how paranoid she is" replied Julia. "We don't know the capacity for targeted individuals to become aware of their monitoring but LJM was aware of the thought machine and there is some evidence from the TM logs that Esther is becoming aware too. Which will presumably lead to paranoia."

"And if that paranoia causes them to seek out their own thought machine, they could suffer the same fate as LJM with the microwaved head. We need to be vigilant to stop that from happening," said Henning.

PUSHING THE LIMITS

MI6 managed to rent a house in the street opposite to Patsy. This was an ideal location for the TM with minimum distance between the observer and the observed. It did mean the neighbours got a good view of the kit being delivered inside the house but they made nothing of it.

Delia turned up in person to supervise its initiation. They were never sure the targeted individual would respond to the TM so it was always a nervous time. Delia knew what to watch out for, with her experience of LJM.

In the event the TM came up with Patsy's stream of thoughts straight away. Delia recognised the familiar patterns and that was the crucial part of the job done.

Now to watch and wait …

The main part of the TM operator's job was immensely tedious. Listening to someone else's stream of consciousness was like watching analogue television with white noise coming down the aerial. Only in certain circumstances could the individual thoughts be pieced together to make a legible whole. The operator would type what he or she thought was the stream of thoughts into a log. This log was then the basis of the analysis done by MI5.

In Patsy's case she was thinking almost constantly so it was difficult for the TM operator to keep up. She was thinking clearly and the sub-vocalisation we all experience as our inner voice was in full flow.

The first area of concern was whether Patsy knew she was being watched. Nothing in her stream of thoughts suggested that she did. However, she made the odd move of coming to the TM house door and knocking on it.

"No, she'll fry her brain," yelled Delia. "I'll pull the plug."

With that she switched off the power to the TM to avert any potential reaction for Patsy.

Interestingly Patsy then lost interest and walked back up the garden path.

So Delia concluded that Patsy was somehow aware of the TM and furthermore knew where it was coming from. This was a level of spookiness not seen with LJM.

LJM visited Patsy to discuss her results. Together they concluded that there was no getting away from the Thought Machine, if that was the best explanation for what was going on. They would each continue to hear voices which were either naturally occurring or man made. However the voices could be controlled by the simple "voices off" thought. Furthermore anti-psychotic medication could be used to push the voices even further into the background.

LJM and Patsy both saw their doctor and were referred to psychiatric care. A range of medication was on offer including olanzapine, quetiapine, depixol, paliperidone and aripiprazole.